SOCCER TALES

SOCCER TALES
LEGEND OF THE SHOELACE MONSTER

written by Lew Freimark

Dance to the Sun Publishers, LLC
CHILDREN'S DIVISION

Soccer Tales – Legend of the Shoelace Monster
  Revised Second Edition • ISBN: 978-0-9993110-5-9
  Copyright ©2018 by Lewis B. Freimark. All rights reserved.

First Edition ©2012 • ISBN: 978-1-61862-949-4

This novel is a work of fiction. Names, descriptions, entities and incidents included in the story are products of the author's imagination. Any resemblance to actual persons, events and entities is entirely coincidental.

The opinions expressed by the author are not necessarily those of
Dance to the Sun Publishers, LLC.

Published by Dance to the Sun Publishers, LLC.
P.O. Box 965, Belle Mead, New Jersey 08502 USA
201-694-9902 | www.soccertales.net

Dance to the Sun Publishers, LLC is committed to excellence in the publishing field. The company has a philosophy that "children come first. They are the future of tomorrow and as educators and publishers we should help them to understand the issues of the day."

Book design copyright ©2018 Dance to the Sun Publishers, LLC. All rights reserved.
Cover and interior design & layout by Bill Thauer / CapeWorksWRT.com
Illustrations by Andrew Seabert
Photographs provided by Lewis Freimark

Published in the United States of America
ISBN: 978-0-9993110-5-9
1. Juvenile Fiction/Sports & Recreation/Soccer
2. Juvenile Fiction/General
18.03.30

DEDICATION

They met over soccer, in a manner of speaking. She was delivering watches to his family; her father was an immigrant watchmaker. He was writhing in pain, lying across a couch. He had just finished a match.

PROSPECT UNITY CLUB OF NEW YORK CITY

They became a fixture at the Prospect Unity Club in New York City. He played fullback on the club team that won the city championship in

1942. Then many members of the team went off to war to fight for their newfound country.

MAX FREIMARK

My father, Max Freimark, was that tough-minded fullback. He taught me about the game of soccer and the discipline needed in life. These immigrants helped America survive the Great Depression and World War II. This book is dedicated to my parents – Max and Gert Freimark – and all the other immigrant soccer players that brought the game to America.

TABLE OF CONTENTS

INTRODUCTION

HOW THE LEGEND BEGAN

"*Psst!* Hey, kids. I'm peeking at you through the tall blades of grass. This is your story. So follow me, the shoelace monster, as I journey to the soccer fields of the good ol' U. S. of A. Don't forget, tie up your laces.

Welcome to the Amazon Rainforest. My baby monster dreams are filled with multicolored soccer laces forming large grinning faces all around me. These laces loop their way across memorable emerald fields of grass. I don't know what this means, only that my fellow baby monsters still laugh at these dreams. I get emails from them even today. Their dreams are different and about scaring kids in the specter of moonlit Halloween nights. Better yet, these monsters are fond of cooking up some potions in a wicked sorcerer's brew. These concoctions change little boys into talking computers or "vice versa, verse vica, or, even worser", forcing little girls into a fondness for broccoli and cauliflower. *Yuch! Blech!*

THE SHOELACE MONSTER

It is a well-known fact that the monster population loves using blood-curdling words *boo! yah! grr!* to scare little kids. I, however, am a different kind of monster. I have always enjoyed strange and exotic words that I keep hearing over and over in my little soccer-ball head. Smiling laces seem to always accompany me deep into the realm of my dreams. I have the fondest memories of the sounds of the *Baio* and the *Ijexa*, a symphony-and-pulse wave of carnival sounds like *de joao, de joao, eh, eh, eh!* These are the mellow sounds I hear that come from long ago in the Amazon Rainforest of Brazil, where a native song of rhythm begins with a drumbeat and the echoing bang of a branch beating on a carved-out log. *Shh*, if you kids listen closely on the soccer field, I bet you can hear that echo in the distance. The rhythms of what we now know as the "Brazilian" style of soccer, 'Ginga' style, are the first musical rhythms I ever heard in my monster life.[1/2]

These are the same rhythms and sounds that the Brazilian players like Neymar, Dani Alves and Lucas Moura hear for themselves on the practice fields of their new home at PSG's training ground of Camp des Loges at Saint-

Germain-en-Laye outside of Paris. They circle around and utter the sound of Woooottt, WOOOOOOO! If you are nearby, you can't help but hear it. It is a noise of exuberance, a noise of joy, a noise that seems delightfully inappropriate for world football's carefully scripted soundtrack.[3]

Every little child of a Brazilian village hears the same sounds and rhythms that I do as they drift and are carried by native musicians as far away as the big city of Rio de Janeiro. Those kids want to lace up a pair of soccer boots and dream a favorite childhood dream of scoring the winning goal with time running out on the game clock. *Five, four, three, two, one—shot. G-O-A-L!*

I always understand that those little boys and girls are destined to be my friends. I tug and pull on their soccer laces once I get to know them. It is hippity-hop fun to stop them from tying up bootlaces, and instead, I loft the rainbow of laces high into the sky while dancing and swaying to the music. Don't you agree that my dreams are a whole lot nicer than scaring little kids like the toads and gnomes take pleasure doing from deep in the Amazon Rainforest?

SOCCER MAKES THE WORLD GO 'ROUND

I am a descendant of countless generations of shoelace monsters. Earliest records place my family in the B.C. China-Mongolian dynasties, where soccer-style matches are played.

My daddy's name is Poppa-Ooh Mow-Mow, and yes, his name becomes famous in lyrics of the 1950's rock-and-roll songs! He always hoists me as a baby up on his knobby, gnarled knees and spins the tales of our family history. He thinks this is my destiny that I am seeing in my dreams. I carry the family legacy to follow the sounds of the boot on ball across the grasslands and urban landscapes of the world. I tug on the global shoelace and bring all the continents together around the game of soccer.

The *xaxado*, a wonderfully rhythmic dance, coupled with the *reco-reco*, a percussive instrument, make the familiar sights and sounds of *de joao, de joao, eh, eh, eh* that we hear mixed into the sounds at the splendidly played 2014 Men's World Cup competition in Brazil! That competition is won by Germany over Argentina, at the Maracana stadium, with a 1-0 stunning overtime goal scoredby Mario Götze.[4]

CHAPTER 1:

THE MONSTER SCHOOL IS CHOCK-FULL OF THE HISTORY OF THE GAME

So now that you have become acquainted with my personality and family history, and, of course, my style on the soccer field, you must be wondering how I develop these super-powers and techniques that have brought me fame in the Amazon Rainforest.

I learned my skills at the Eenie-Meenie-Miney-Mo Monster School on Gobbledy Guck Lane. These days I still take refresher courses on line with the school.

My daddy, Poppa-Ooh-Mow-Mow, is the headmaster of the school. He teaches many of the courses himself, such as the basics: lace twirling, yanking and pulling, spinning and riding, peek-a-boo 101, and the cling-on independent study. These courses are designed to teach successive generations of shoelace monsters how to hang on to laces and avoid being caught by munchkin-size soccer players.

EENIE-MEENEY-MINEY-MO SCHOOL
ON GOBBLEDLY GUCK LANE
Monsters Rule
Handy Dandy Handbook

The cling-on is my most difficult course because it takes many months to perfect my ball-clinging techniques. You have to use paw suction power to grip the soccer ball and then hang on for dear life as the ball spins to and fro. My favorite type of ball is the old leather casers where a panel is loose or frayed. When I cling on to these flaps, it provides me with natural camouflage from the kids.

Now, I look back with fond memories on graduation night. I invited all the gremlins, ghouls, trolls, gibbledees and gobbledoos in the neighborhood to participate in the festivities. Deep into the night as the moon's beams are absorbed by the forest, the party carries on and the fire's flames cast their magic onto all monsterdom.

Poppa tells me I am, as part of my education, going to undergo physical training to learn my skills as a novice lace puller. Growing up, I can only groan and sigh as I yank and tug to pop open the laces. Poppa says that the real challenge, the real test for the kids, is to continue to play on despite this obstacle. The passion of soccer is really on parade when little kids play through my tricks and traps. Many times I just plain plop on my rear end straining to learn what Poppa teaches me. Poppa warns me to be a determined little fellow, and I learn my lessons well. He always teaches us that it is the force of the soccer legends that holds that giant global shoelace high in the sky. It is an offering to them. But he also tells me that even with the laces untied, these boys and girls will never stop playing their beloved game of soccer.

As I grow older, stronger, and wiser and graduate to earn my diploma, the rhythms and sounds of soccer spread throughout all of South America and to the countries of North America, and I again follow the bouncing beat and sounds of *de joao, de joao, eh, eh, eh* up the coasts of Central America, Mexico, and the United States.

Historically, did you know that soccer comes to Brazil, as told through the story of a man named Miller? Mr. Miller comes to Brazil from England and works in building the railroad in São Paulo. These events occur in the last decades of the nineteenth century. Mr. Miller sends his son, Charlie, back to England to get his general education, and it is in England that Charlie learns to play the organized style of soccer. He becomes a master of the dribble, serve, feint, use of rapid speed, heading, and crossing. He begins playing for top club teams in England.[5]

Charles Miller, Father of Modern Brazilian Football.

When he returns to São Paulo, he brings the organized game with him and helps to develop now-famous teams, such as the Corinthians and São Paulo Club teams (SPAC) of Brazil, teaching them the necessary skills from which the locals develop their own flair, style, and verve. This Brazilian style, "Ginga" is what gives Brazilian futbol players their fluidity and rhythm on the soccer pitch and enables them to *'Joga Bonito'* (Play Beautiful.) See the youtube video that depicts "Ginga."[6] All countries are indebted to the Brazilian culture of soccer. The rest of the international soccer community and those of us in Monster Land are equally indebted to Brazil for its soccer legacy and style. Look to the festivities of Brazilian Rio Carnival which is a wild 5-day celebration reflecting the style and culture of Brazil. In 2018 it did occurr most recently from February 9-14.

In fact, the 2002 men's World Cup competition, as it unfolds, reveals some of the brilliance of the Brazilian style of play as they reach and succeed in the tournament final.[7] These Brazilians of Pele, Carlos Alberto, Rivaldo, Cafu, Ronaldinho and Antônio Rinaldo Gonçalves, are five-time champions, and the Germans have successfully won four titles.[8]

CHAPTER 2:

FRIENDS, FRIENDS, AND MORE FRIENDS (YOU CAN NEVER HAVE ENOUGH OF THEM!)

Naturally I excel at Monster School and I begin my journey to carry the message of soccer to the farthest corners of the world. I begin traveling north through the wild grass fields of South and Central America and come, at last, upon the youth soccer teams in today's U.S.A. I begin thinking to myself:

My, my, my, I love this rich, fertile, grassy ground. I can sure grab up some shoelaces and challenge these kids to play on. Look at the little boys and girls running on the fields with their colorful uniforms and shiny new cleats. I think this is really what my baby dreams are all about. These children love my sport of soccer and are the future of my game.

I cross my arms and fix a determined smile upon my face, "Where they go, it is my destiny to follow."

These children are far luckier than some of those street kids I meet in the urban concrete landscape or in poor, rural farm areas. Many times these kids are playing with no sneakers or with sneakers that are all torn up. I will have a lot more to say in a later chapter about "Flashing" Dervin and his mates, the underprivileged street kids I encounter at the Brickies Soccer Academy and the wonderful bus rides home we share.

In *Soccer Tales II – Born to Play the Game*, I recount how Coach Stu comes to practices with bags of used cleats to try to match up the high school girls' shoe sizes because they cannot afford to buy new cleats. Hey, what about these poor little Russian kids in *Soccer Tales III – Baba Yaga's Revenge*? All of their soccer balls have gotten stolen by the witch, Baba Yaga. She is driven by her dislike of the game of soccer and she is attempting to ruin the 2018 Men's World Cup in Russia. Read that story, if you dare not to be scared of witches. Find out the fate of these Russian kids as they enlist the aid of my Shoo-Crew in their quest to retrieve their soccer balls. Those of us who love the game still want the upcoming tournament to be played.

Most of the kids in North America, who can afford new cleats have all kinds of laces to pick from for their soccer cleats, since the shoe companies of the Zaps, Big Prowlers, and other logos use different kinds of laces for each of their shoes.

In addition as to the two colors of cleats you see players wearing today, the explanation simply put is that the boots are designed to be different colors. There are two different shoe models, one type designed for running speed and the other for shooting power. Each type is sold as a pair, so a player who wants to mix the two types must buy both pairs.[9]

Also, take note that the British coaches and trainers say the English leagues teach the kids to undertie the shoelaces beneath the cleats—they feel the longest laces, like seventy-two inches, are the best to have. Other coaches from different countries feel differently, but it doesn't bother me because I know how to use my muscles now in order to tug real hard. Once I grab and zero in on the laces I want, I can sway and swoop to the rhythms of the beat, which are woven into the fabric and tradition of the game of soccer.

During these practices, I never allow myself to be captured. NEVER, NEVER, NEVAHH!! I just peek out through the blades of grass like a spy ready to pounce. Once I have my victims in sight, they become part of my Shoo-Crew list of favorite players. I will definitely continue to yank and tug on their laces. Parents and coaches know the kids I'm talking about – the ones whose laces are always untied. Coaches, parents, and side-line observers can identify with the phenomena of the floppy laces. It takes a special kind of kid who will continue to play soccer despite the flopping of laces. Many times these are the same kids who, early on in their soccer careers, can be standing idly by on the field away from the action or running the wrong way when they finally do get the ball on their feet. We all know these kids – the ones who are daydreamers and flower pickers, always falling down because their motor skills are not, at this stage, as developed as the other children.

Hey, here are stories from my classic kid collection of antics. I know a child who tries to see if a quarter will fit up his nose. Not recommended for good health. Then there is another young lad who has the habit of swinging from the chandelier cord at home – another no-no! There are the kids who are dirt magnets. Kids like these are always digging in the dirt with a stick or are discovering grasshoppers and garter snakes.

Jake, Koga, and Jay are some of these kids, and they become my best friends throughout their five seasons with me. I will introduce them to you further throughout these pages. No matter how tight these guys tie their laces, I swoop and sneak in with little puffs of smoke coming off my feet. I dive in, untie them, and escape without being detected. I am just that kind of fast and crafty!

I roll over in chuckles and the adults become puzzled. That's what I'm all about, **chuckles and puzzles**! You know that despite the fact that their children's laces and shoes are loose all the time it never crosses the kids' minds to worry about these flip-floppy laces because they play on with passion for the game. Truly that is what it is all about and it should be that way.

I've been described by my family and friends as teeny and tiny. I'm also quite exquisitely cuddly. Look out soccer world, here I come! I am not at all like some of the gruesome monsters I have grown up with and still know back in the Brazilian jungles and forest. I have perfectly round, big, and bulgy eyes and nice eyebrows too. Sometimes I like to wear sports platinum fronts on my perfectly formed teeth and display dragon and eagle tattoos. Sometimes I add a bowtie made of shoelaces for a nice touch to my wardrobe. But as cute as I am, very few, if any, of the little children can see me hiding below the blades of grass on the field. The last thing I would ever want to have happen is to scare a little child from playing soccer. Some of the kids claim they see a small shadowy figure scurrying in the grass and under their cleats but that it moves so fast they aren't able to catch it. Most of the parents think it's just the kids' imagination. Also, despite the laces flying in the breeze or being grabbed by me, this does not stop the kids from playing their beloved soccer games.

Kids, the only thing I can warn you about is to keep your eyes open and stay alert while you play because you may be able to catch a glimpse of *moi* as I'm pulling pranks. *Moi*, ha ha!

CHAPTER 3:

HOMETOWN USA

Summer is zapping its way to the finish line in the town of Smudgeville. These are the suburbs of our good ol' U.S. of A. It is that time of year when kids think the days are moving by with the blink of an eye and the image of school days and homework loom in the not-too-distant future. The children are returning from camp and shopping in the local sports stores, looking for the right size and color of soccer cleats to complement their uniforms for the fall soccer season. At least for the kids, the start of soccer season makes the beginning of the school year much easier to handle.

The design, colors, and styles of soccer cleats parallel the development of the soccer ball and the history of the game. I have never seen as many color cleats as are now out there on the shelves. These new prowler-style cleats are streamlined, and allow the player's foot to feel the ball better.

This design technology supposedly improves the manner in which the kids can kick the ball. The old hobnail miner's boots (leather, high-topped boot) had a blunt, slightly upturned toe end. These older boots were heavier back then, so it was possible to exert enormous force behind even a heavy ball to kick it a long distance.[10] The newer prowler, or cheetah type of cleat, is claimed by the manufacturers to make the ball dip and swerve with more velocity than the more traditional boot.[11]

Jake is one of these soccer kids in Smudgeville, and he makes up his mind to have a pair of cleats with red trim because his team, the Vipers, have always worn red jerseys, and this particular year is no different. In order to complete his uniform, Jake matches those wonderful sports goggles in the same red uniform color. You'll see he is regally clad in many of the pictures that I have made part of my story. His team has been together for a number of years and always has "extreme, mad" fun during the soccer season. The players and parents on the team always talk about the time Thomas's dog, Chelsea, a golden retriever, was stopping shots in the goal with her paws. The Vipers are always on the lookout for good goalkeepers, and a team joke is that someday when things get desperate and the team needs to hold a lead, Chelsea will come trotting out to the nets, wagging her tail!

Also, funny stuff seems to always happen to the kids on this team at their practices and games. I can also do some pretty strange or, as the kids say, *whack* things, but this team even outdoes me. I love it! This shooie-chewie shoelace monster likes teams with kooky chemistry. For example, there is the time when the team was watching the skyrockets and fireworks, which some adults are launching hundreds of feet into the air, over our practice field in the park. Those rockets soar into the sky with so much noise and light that it is impossible to keep playing ball without running over there to see the launch pad. Even Coach Stu stops the training and allows the boys to take a break to see these rockets.

I remember another ruckus that descends on a particular practice afternoon. One of the babysitters is sitting in her car, and she and her boyfriend are rumored to be "smooching it up." Another driver, who is not looking, crashes into the rear end of this love mobile. Luckily, nobody

THE SQUIRTMASTER

is hurt, but the sound it makes to us is like a magnitude 10 on the earthquake scale. All the boys have to run and see what happened. The babysitter and her boyfriend are really embarrassed! For the rest of the season, that babysitter never lives it down – ooh, ooh, kissy, kissy. One thing about Viper practices – there never is a dull moment!

Another fun thing the children enjoyed is what the Vipers call the "Squirtmaster," a water-spraying, squirting, and misting machine that we use in these humid days of the late spring and early fall. It always feels so good to the players to be able to spray themselves down with the nozzle in the middle of practice. A scrimmage can really make a player hot, and the "Squirtmaster's" stream of cool water is a welcome break. The kids and I think that the water from it is even better than all that bottled water everyone carries around with them these days. Coach Stu admits to the kids that the Squirtmaster water just comes from the outside faucet at his house, but nobody cares. I think the water tastes as good as some of the best mountain streams in the rainforest. Most parents probably have their own fond memories of water from the outside tap when they were kids.

Mark is another one of my favorite kids. He totally soaks himself spraying the Squirtmaster. Also, his shinguards are always dangling any which way. He typically wears a T-shirt in the cold fall season practices, which results in doses of sniffles and sneezes during the season. Parents be wary of these kids especially during flu season Usually there is one or two on every team. They are the snifflers, and they usually have to be carried off the field kicking and screaming before they will put a dry shirt on!

Despite all of his quirks, Mark keeps improving, and in one pivotal year, he scores the second goal of his career. It is a thing of beauty in its pursuit and stick-to-it-ivity. Mark pounces on the loose ball and dribbles toward the goal, where his kick just catches the near side of the net. Unfortunately, this was Mark's last year with the Vipers because he moves to another town. I think we all will miss his spirit and the pure joy of his game. Good-bye, my friend, and may the thud of boot on ball stay with you.

It is common knowledge among Vipers that Coach Stu's bark is worse than his bite. He should come to the rainforest and compete with the howls of the wolves at night or my goblin friends. The best howling I still hear echoing through my memories all the way down to my toes was done by my friend Enoch, the werewolf. When I go back to visit the rainforest, especially for the 2014 Men's World Cup, Enoch is still screaming over the treetops for hours keeping everybody awake. Did you ever hear a little red fox scream? Check out Internet videos. I bet you will be surprised at how loud they can get. Now you can just imagine how my friends sound in the rainforest!!

But really, Coach Stu is a softie. He said that if any of the players continue to be disruptive, he will issue that player a red card, and send him to the sideline during practice. The red card is a red plastic toy he keeps in his pocket. A lot of kids try to pick that pocket during the practice scrimmage to get the red card away from him - a sort of "*Grand Theft Red Card.*" Of course, you can imagine that when Coach Stu reaches for the game piece to issue the red card, it won't be there. Ha-ha! It is funny to see his face when he realizes the red card is missing! His face gets as red as that card. It's a way the kids say they can keep coach. real. We all have a "real" chuckle over that one.

The first season this team assembles for play as seven – to eight-year-olds, there are very few skilled players that can help the team score goals. These early Vipers specialize in what Coach Stu calls the "clumping phenomenon." Clumping is defined as a bunch of anything that sticks together, whether intended or not. This consists, in the case of the Vipers, of a whole group of players hovering around the ball and trying their hardest to kick or move it along. If the team is lucky enough to have the ball plop or pop out of the clump onto the foot of one of our players and toward the opposition's goal, then we might be lucky enough to score. Unfortunately for my favorite little team in this their first season, they rarely are able to declumpify and score many goals. More times than not it is like a mass of little human bodies moving as one big ball surrounding a little soccer ball.

Also, another point you can count on happening at least a couple of times a game is that some of the kids get totally confused about which direction to kick the ball, forgetting which side of the field they are attacking. Coaches and parents should understand that, for beginners in soccer or organized sports, this is not unusual but rather pretty normal as kids get used to the flow of the game. Above all else, we should be patient with our kids, let them grow into their skills and always remember to give them positive support.

Sometimes kids are not as aggressive or are lacking in concentration. Parents should not get upset when they see their kids picking up and throwing grass at each other instead of competing for control of the ball.

> "Coach Stu really tries to coax them and get them to participate. He can often be overheard saying, "Let's not have any press conferences out there on the field. Parents, just remember that these are little people playing soccer, not World Cup or MLS competitions. Parents, coaches, and grandparents, be patient and maybe through our efforts as coaches and parents we will develop a few stars of the future, but most of the kids should just have plain old fun."

The first season we are fortunate not to lose by even greater scores than we do. Notice I say "we" because I consider myself to be an integral part of the Vipers. I am here for them, even though they don't know it. Like their spirit, I hover around them, giving love and attention to their shoelaces, of course.

This brings to mind one little defender, Julio, whose skill is to kick every ball that is on his side of the field out-of-bounds. Man, he is like a robot. Kick it out, kick it out, kick it out, little Julio! He knows only this particular tactic and does the skill well with vim, gusto and passion. It is a real blessing for our team. Julio pays no heed to kicking the ball up the field, but that is okay since, for us, out-of-bounds is better than in the nets against us! He is a smart cookie that way and always knows and calculates that doing this skill will work okay for him and the team.

Another thing that Coach Stu insists on that Jake really thinks is so neat is to make sure that no one yells at our goalkeepers. At this age let's face it nobody wants to play goal-keeper. Come on, ask yourself would a normal and emotionally balanced person realistically take on this job? Of course I am kidding, but my favorite goalies are always a little off in personality! First of all, it takes oodles and gobs of courage to get between those "pipes." If anyone yells at one of our goal-keepers for allowing any goals, Coach will pull that player off the field for poor sportsmanship. Coach Stu says, "Above all else, defense is what wins games, and we never yell at our last line of defense, the keeper!" This makes all our goalkeepers feel protected and gives them support in this most difficult position on the field. When you're a striker you can take a dozen shots per game and not get blamed too much. Score one and you can be a hero. Second, the risk about being a keeper is that the keeper is always visible. He or she has no teammates around them when the shot is taken, especially on breakaways. They are on center stage and visible to all the spectators and players on the field. Third, it can be a lonely position filled with minutes of standing alone, followed by instantaneous flows of action when shots are taken or breakaways created with players bearing down on goal. There is great glory or instant doom in those moments when shots are taken. Jake thinks that great goalies have courage and un-usually quirky personalities. They consider the goal area to be their home, and they guard it jealously. Some of them stake the goal area out, scratching it up with their cleats if the referees

MATTY'S ICE CREAM WAR

don't give them a penalty for unsportsmanlike conduct. This territoriality is part of the ritual associated with being a keeper. They also make themselves ever more visible since they are required to wear special color jerseys that differ from the team color. Wearing a different hue makes a fashion statement on the field. Part of a keeper's personality is the type and color of uniform they choose to wear.

One of my favorite goalkeepers on the Vipers is Matty. He is able to shrug off goals with a smile and a joke. He will resume his courageous position in the net or "the old potato sack," as the true-blue, old-school soccer fans call it. As an example of his quirkiness, when Matty goes to a birthday party he is seen talking to his parachute soldiers, which he places, on a whim, in the big scoops of ice cream in his sundae. This is Matty just being Matty, having an ordinary conversation between toy soldiers. One of the other kids calls him a moron and Matty's reply, with a smile, is, "Great, I'm a moron. I'm a moron!" You gotta love him! That's the kind of personality that the coach says makes a great keeper. What do you think?

The Vipers in this first year have a lot of other wacky and quirky personalities among the players. First of all, there is Daniel. He can be a difficult child for Coach Stu to work with because he is usually doing something else rather than listening to the coach's instructions. I still think he reminds me of a Snimbach from the mountain area on the edge of my jungle. Snimbachs don't like to listen to advice either, especially when you need to give instructions to them on how to climb the high mountain passes. Most of the time, Daniel is knocking people down during the scrimmages. And it isn't as if he is a bad kid; he just seems to like the physical contact during games. Maybe it is because his family is from Australia where they play Australian rules of football. For whatever reason, this is Daniel's style and sometimes it leads to embarrassing moments for the team. One team opponent in this first year refuses to come out for the second half of a game unless Daniel stops knocking players down. Their coaches approach the ref, point to Daniel, and say, "That kid cannot roughhouse our kids anymore or we will walk off the field!"

Coach Stu frequently has to get Daniel to promise to stop doing this or games will be forfeited. Daniel is a great kid, and Coach always feels that Daniel will turn out to be a serious player. Daniel does progress as the seasons moved along. Daniel can exhaust Coach Stu and the team's patience. We remember him telling new players joining the Vipers for a season "not to worry about Coach's red cards because Coach doesn't keep you on the bench for too long if he gives you one." But Daniel is always part of our team, and we accept and back him up. Daniel also is one of those quirky and fierce goalkeepers the Vipers usually discover from within their ranks and he makes many tremendous saves for us during the seasons. He is a fine punter whose kicks are used as an offensive weapon to spring a striker loose for an attack on the opposition's goal.

The Vipers goal-keeping corps changes in the years that follow. Daniel is replaced by Peter, who frequently gets into fights with his team-mates during practices. He and Ethan tangle all the time and, just like Daniel, this seems to be an extension of his need for physical contact on the soccer field. Ethan is also a real character among the players. He struts around as an aggressive little player. He walks on to the team, although no one seems to know him because he is a year

SOCCER-PLAYING CHICKEN

behind in school from most of the other players. I will certainly talk more about Ethan in these tales. Getting back to Peter, in one memorable week at practice, Peter, in a display of his fighting spirit, bites Siggy in the leg when he scores on him and they have an old-fashioned rumble which has to be broken up by Coach. Siggy is quoted as saying he is going to "get that old piece of chicken and put him in the refrigerator!" We're still trying to figure out what that means.

Kids make constant reference to chickens: "You are a chicken!" or "You are a chicken bone!" or "You big piece of chicken nugget!" So I have written a rap, which I call "Chicken and Lace."

> *My name is the shoelace monsta, yo, yo.*
> *My name is the shoelace monsta, yo, yo.*
> *But I don't live in no dumpsta, no, no.*
>
> *I loosen kids' laces.*
> *And see joy on their faces.*
>
> *But chickens are perplexin.'*
> *Only kids can put the hex on.*
>
> *I don't get it 'cause it's complexin'*
> *And quite a bit vexin.'*
>
> *If you know the answer, please text me,*
> *Even down here in Shoelace Monsta land!*

CLEATS AHOY KOGA!

After spewing forth all these chicken references, Coach has to calm Siggy down and by the end of practice, Peter and Siggy are talking again and Peter is saying how his dad is going to come to the game on Saturday with red spray paint and spray anyone who wants red hair – the Viper color.

Another one of my favorites is Daniel's friend, Koga. Koga is a special kid with a shy personality. This kid is really like a quiet autumn breeze. He never has a bad word to say to anyone yet rarely smiles. But when he does smile it lights up your heart. He is all arms and gangly legs, like a windmill. He is gifted with a lot of natural speed, but many times in our early seasons, he will be flailing and missing at the ball and almost always tumbling over by trying so hard. Inevitably, his cleats can be spotted flying high in the air. He just needs to develop the right skills. Apparently he's still working with shoes, as we find out at the Viper reunion. He works as a shoe salesman. He's still trying hard!

For sure, Koga becomes one of my favorite targets. Players like Koga fuel my legend with their stories. Koga is a Haitian child. I think his French is better than his English, and sometimes he does not seem able to translate instructions clearly. No matter, because he loves the game despite whatever roadblocks I can throw in his path. No one can remember when Koga's laces are ever completely tied. It seems like every time you glance his way his laces are always loose! Thank you, thank you, I will take my bows now! Whether in the outdoor or indoor seasons, Koga is my little cookie-faced kid. Koga's cleats and laces are constantly sailing out over the field. No one on the field can ever understand this because Koga insists that he ties them tight before every practice. I have always been just too fast for everybody, tee hee, tee hee. Somehow the laces are already loose when practice gets underway. The mystery of Koga's cleats continues on for five years of Viper soccer

Whee! One time, Jay and Koga both have their surplus of laces hanging out along the ground from my tugs and yanks. Jay's parents warn him to tie em up, and Jay just tucks all the extra laces into the heel of his boot. That's not a good hiding place from my little fingers. I merely jump onto his cleats and pull them out again while hanging on to those laces as they go flopping around in the wind. Can you believe that a few minutes later Jay assists on a goal by Renny that appears to be the game-winning goal! This is the stuff that legends are made of. My kids and I are in that soccer rhythm together, *de joao, de joao, eh, eh, eh,* and when we are like that nothing can stop us!

Girls are welcome in my group, especially in the winter's indoor season, because that's when the kids play co-ed soccer. Later in the recreational league, and when the kids get to middle school, the outdoor leagues have girls and boys playing on the same teams. Allie is one of the best girls to twirl laces on. I like grabbing on to her long hair while she is sitting on the sidelines. You have to see her face after I do a braid or two and she just can't understand how she gets that hairstyle.

This is really funny, and the look on her mother's face is even more hysterical as she exclaims, "Allie, which one of your friends braided your hair?" and Allie's typical response is, "Mom, I don't know. I am just watching the game."

Getting back to the Renny goal and the circumstances surrounding it which turns it into

an upsetting event because there lurks an evil wizardess referee – we call her the "Grinchess Referee"– on the playing fields of Smudgeville. She is a friend of the league commissioner, and we call him the Big Commish. His real name is Reginald C. Grumpf. Those two almost certainly qualify for the "Grumpy" award given out to the most miserable monsters in the rainforest. She misses so many calls and he supports her most of the time, trying to act like a bigshot scary monster. For instance, she calls offsides several minutes (a l-o-n-g several minutes!) after the Renny play is over. How outrageous to do this with eight and nine-year-olds! It makes the game ultimately end in a 0-0 tie. Jay is heart-broken and crying. The Viper parents are very upset! Coach Stu walks out to talk with the referee. Her buddy, the Big Commish, also quickly comes off the sideline to put in his two cents. Coach Stu in a clear way and controlling his temper points out that the rules of this league state that no offsides at this age shall be called unless it is a blatant offense. This particular play should not even remotely be called offsides. Renny is clearly in an onside position when the play begins as a result of Jay's hustle. He has a defender

THE GRINCHESS REFEREE AND THE BIG COMMISH

between him in the goal, and he does not create an advantage for himself or interfere with the play. This is the rule! Ms. Grinchy-Face wrongly determines the outcome of the game on a very close call and obviously makes the call much too late. All of us agree, as a team, to not accept the tie and to file a complaint with the league. We just call it a win for our team, and since the league does not keep standings anyway for our kids' age bracket it makes the lads feel good to know they have stood up against an injustice.

My Viper kids have inherited through me all of my family's rhythms and beats of salsa and samba soccer music flowing through their blood from South America. However, you have to understand that the game of soccer has certainly changed its personality. It is much different from the style of game that came from England and the Blackburn Rovers, the original team of organized soccer at the turn of the twentieth century.[12]

The game has evolved into various styles, one of which is the short passing and dribbling style of Pele (Edson Arantes dos Nascimento). If you can say his full name three times fast, you should

First known photo of Blackburn Rovers, 1875.

win a prize from your coach, parents, yes, maybe? Also, make note of his 'smooth as silk' teammate, Carlos Alberto of that same Santos Club and the Brazilian men's World Cup teams of 1958 and the later 2002 champion.[13]

Koga is chosen as a prime victim by me because he fits in with the rhythms of the rainforest. Jake's older brother, Jase, said that on his travel team, which is a state championship team, they also have a kid whose laces are always playing loose and free but he plays the game well with his laces trailing behind. Little did they know that I am an equal opportunity lace puller and do not discriminate at any level of soccer skill. Another reason I go for teams like the Vipers is that they are a multicultural team where I can feel the beat of music drawn from many different countries and cultures. The first Viper team had children from French-Canada, Haiti, China, Pakistan, Australia, Mexico, Portugal, and, of course, the United States, and this makes the team all the more interesting for me. I alway feel at home with all these languages being spoken, since my family history shows us crossing many continents until I arrive in America.

Now here's a description of some of the tools of my trade, never before revealed to the public, a virtual skill set for soccer monsters. For $19.95, in just four easy payments, you can own my catalog of chaos! It's a joke I'm playing with you, kiddies! I have perfected shoelace trickery into a science, just like Poppa Ooh Mow-Mow taught me. I launch myself out on the field, scurrying around, flitting behind long blades of grass to get a good view of the players. Next, I proceed to target my player selections for the season. Sometimes with the fields in bad condition from rain and not being cared for properly, I can dive into a muddy field and camouflage my appearance into a big old mud ball. I then swim to my target and latch onto the laces that way. It's hard to see me with the mud caked all over my little monster body. Guess what? I can even do the backstroke or swim like a submarine in or below the mud puddles—one, two, three, four! I also hunt the urban street fields of "the hood," in places like The Brickies Academy or the communities that have better fields with soft, green grass. I think the kids who play on the hard concrete and urban landscapes are even more heroic because the pavement can be so unforgiving when you fall. Most of The Brickies Academy kids just pop up, dust themselves off, scraped knees and all, and keep playing. It's because they have accepted my challenge to play on for the love of the game! In America, we have to recognize that some of our greatest raw talent comes out of these poor neighborhoods and needs to be developed through our youth soccer development programs.

In America, I always feel like a cowboy riding the laces in the old Wild West turning them into a lasso throughout the soccer season. Yee-haw, ride 'em cowboy! If one is lucky enough to spot me out on the field, you might catch a glimpse while I pull and tug on the laces gripping the ends firmly between my teeth. I will stuff as much of the laces into my puffy pouches until the knot pops open. What a funky sight. In the future, I feel it can become a TV reality show about me called "You Are the Grossest Link!" Imagine me starring on this show while stuffing the laces and making the grossest face.

To be fair, the other competitors would be given a break by allowing them to stuff marshmallows into their mouths, noses, and ears and competing with their own puffy faces. We're talking high ratings for this show. It will be a winner!

Let's now talk some more of the action-packed Viper history. The first Viper season the team endures a multiple number of losses and manages a few ties with other teams. A few of the losses are blowouts because the other teams are so much more skilled or faster than our lads. Coach knows that we have to get our team conditioned for play on the larger fields. It is our first experience on these fields. Believe me, it is really a big step up. In fact, some of the kids remark "that the field is endless and we need telescopes to see

Grossest
Link!

the other goal!" There certainly are a lot of hanging tongues forcing substitutions to be made, but the kids work hard at the weekly practices to condition themselves for the full-sided field. The team record shows a positive upward curve as the Vipers only lose one or two games by season number three. We definitely begin to see progress in their skills and fitness.

The first season really is funny with me pulling out the laces, the kids daydreaming games away, and a bunch of other characters joining up with the team. Ethan was previously introduced to you in my story. Coach always calls him "Pappy." He calls him that because a few times he comes to practice wearing a sailor's cap and dangling a fake corncob pipe from his mouth. He also walks with his forearms out. Ethan is a very aggressive but extremely bright child. His mom says he suffers from ADD / AD / HD (Attention Deficit / Hyperactivity Disorder), and he certainly has difficulty concentrating on instructions. "Pappy, don't climb up on that batting cage!" "Pappy, stop wrestling with Daniel!" Boy do I remember well coach's frustration with Ethan. Ethan is always in the mix and fighting for the ball. In fact, Ethan is the only kid I've heard of, who gets suspended from preschool for scrapping with another kid. The battles between Daniel and Ethan are epic in the Viper chronicles. One time he fights Daniel who is picking on another teammate, Joey. Joey is Ethan's best friend. Ethan grabs a soccer ball and throws it right at Daniel's head, telling him, "No one picks on my friend!" Fortunately, Daniel is not hurt. Obviously, Ethan is very loyal to his friends, and he and Daniel have to be pulled apart frequently during the first couple of seasons. They have ironed out their differences over the years and actually play on a travel team together in another town some seasons later. It is just that they are fiercely competitive and physical players.

Ethan is built like a fireplug usually seen bouncing around the field. Most of the time Ethan pops out of a pack of players and wins the ball. His low center of gravity allows him to stay on his feet and make an attack on goal. We love him on the team for all his energy and excitement, and Ethan really relishes being part of the Vipers. He later becomes a pretty good high school wrestler and that is understandable based on the grit he shows for the Vipers. One year, because of the league rules and player selection, Ethan transfers over to another team with yellow jerseys. He says it didn't feel right to be wearing another uniform and playing against the Vipers. Ethan and his mom say it is a most uncomfortable season for them and he enjoys being back with the team.

Ethan is so happy when the parents organize the first five-year Viper reunion party. A number of parents plan this party, and some of the players from former years are in attendance. Even to this day, we are still having reunion parties. The Vipers will always be a bunch of wild party animals! One coach who nobody wants to invite to any of our parties is the one that coach Stu asked to tone down his yelling at the games. His ridiculous and mean-spirited reply to Coach is that "these ten-year-olds will be men someday and they need to learn #*$#*." Geesh, not another grouch! Guys like him carry their clipboards, or uPid 2's, around, like the Big Commish, trying to act like hotshots. Ironically, Coach Stu is reffing a game a few weeks later with me by his side, along with a group of wonderful eight year old players. One of the coaches has an uPid 2 in his hands presumably for charting the shots taken by his team. The problem is he never uses it during the game and never even sets it down on the ground. He just carries it around to probably make himself look important, and who cares, really? These are eight-year-olds putting on a marvelous display of soccer and sportsmanship – a very clean and well-played game. I don't think you can ask for anything more than that, so why bother with the technology, at least at this age?

Mark is also loyal to our team. We recall how, in the first losing season, he, as our goalie, cries when the other teams score on him, and Coach has to sit him down and talk about how things will get better. Lo and behold, we begin to win late in the second season. By the third season, this improvement translates into a number of wins and skill development and by the spring season – we only lose a couple of games. The children also make great friendships that have endured after the last soccer ball is rolled out for the season. On the Vipers, for instance, at least five of the boys are in the same Cub Scout den and a number attend the same school. This is wonderful stuff because it allows friendships to

Anyway, all of this is getting too serious, so let's bring it back to me and see what kind of mayhem and shenanigans I play on my kids next. I mean, I always make a habit of finding a bunch of wonderful hiding places on a soccer field. Just think about it. Coach brings cones and discs, balls of all sizes, water bottles, and medical kits to our practices. All of these are perfect places for me to hide behind and wait for the opportunity to grab a handful of some laces. Memory recalls that old gnarled tree, a familiar friend on the field at practice. This tree hangs with us for all five years that we practice in the park. Also, by the rules of soccer, a tree is a natural object and, as such, it is considered part of the field. It has these low branches that give me cover to run underneath, and the tree trunk is three to four feet wide. You cannot even spot me in its crevices. So an unsuspecting player, like Koga, has little defense against my monster lace assaults. The sounds of the drumbeat and salsa music always back me up as I flit and hide. It doesn't matter whether there is rain, sunshine, or mud. I have the dreams of smiling, grinning laces jumping all through my mind, and I will be thinking of all the days gone by and the great heroes of my sport.

I remember vividly the images Poppa describes about the early days of soccer. He paints a picture for me of the ancient soccer games from the Chinese Dynasties where it is said Cuju was developed. It means "kick the ball with foot." It was a popular sport played by ancient Chinese, which is similar to today's soccer game.

Ancient History of Soccer

During the Warring States Period (476-221 BC), Cuju was used as fitness training for military cavaliers. The popularity of Cuju spread from the army to the royal courts and upper classes in the Han Dynasty (206 BC-220 AD). It is said that the Han emperor Wu Di enjoyed the sport very much, and matches were often held inside the imperial palace. It was also during the Han Dynasty that Cuju games were standardized and rules were established. A type of court called Ju Chang was built especially for Cuju matches, which had six crescent-shaped goal posts at each end.

The sport was developed during the Tang Dynasty (618-907), when the feather-stuffed ball was replaced by an air-filled ball with a two-layered hull.[14]

In another part of the world, the empires of the Mayans and Aztecs of Mexico and the Americas played similar competitions. They held these matches on huge grass fields which still exist today and were great events where warriors proved their skills and endurance. It was called Ullamaliztli, the famous Aztec ball game, was played on a tlachtli ball court (the game is sometimes referred to as Tlachtli). The ball court was one of the first things built when the Aztecs settled a new area, making it the most important of the ancient Aztec games. It was a very difficult game played with a large rubber ball (the name of the game comes from the word ulli, or rubber). The game was not just important for entertainment, but also politics and religion.[15]

I now show you one of my prized possessions this crinkled-up, old black-and-white picture of the Blackburn Rovers, the first team of organized soccer from England,[16] and the club team that US goalie Brad Friedel played for admirably in past years.[17]

First known photo of Blackburn Rovers, 1875.

What about the great Uruguayan men's World Cup teams of the 1950s? That Uruguayan squad didn't do badly in 2010 either, coming in third place in the tournament. This is the country that invented Futsal, or the five versus five indoor soccer game.[18] Let's not forget the Chinese, Polish, and French teams in the 1998 and 2002 men's World Cups.[19] This monster is so impressed with the play of the super French team of Zinidene Zidane until he loses his cool and his "mind" by head butting the Italian defender, Marco Matterazi in the 2006 men's World Cup.[20] On the opposite side of the ball in that tournament is Fabio Cannavaro, the rock and bull-like defender. He turns back most of the French advances and for his efforts is awarded the *Ballon d'Or*, or the Golden Ball, by FIFA, the international governing body of football.[21]

The thing that always impresses me and the fans about the French team, is the varied styles that they are capable of playing. In the men's World Cup of 1998, it could be seen that they play with both an aggressive attacking style, as well as a counterattacking style. This strategy amounts to waiting for the other teams to make errors and then pouncing on those mistakes to score goals. Zidane's brilliant midfield play in setting up his teammates with passes timed right on their feet, along with the solid goaltending of Fabian Barthez, keep the team in most games and on their way to the 1998 title.[22] Coach predicts that the French style is the style of the future in soccer. The team that is smart and can vary its style of play based on its opponent's weaknesses will, more times than not, prove victorious.

The 2000 European Cup final of France and Italy ends in a golden goal overtime victory for France and is an amazingly exciting final match. Thierry Henri develops into a supreme striker capable of aggressively using his blazing speed to score goals.[23] This varied style of play is now taken up by surprise teams like Senegal, "The Lions of Dakar," South Korea, Turkey, and, we hope, the U.S.A. for the 2022 World Cup.[24]

The debacle of the United States losing to Trinidad and Tobago and being disqualified from this year's Men's World Cup is chronicled in *Soccer Tales III – Baba Yaga's Revenge* and *The Soccer Tales Coloring Book – U.S. Soccer Reset* also published by Dance to the Sun Publishers, LLC.

One historical reference I'm going to make right now is to the 2010 Euro Cup champions of Barcelona, Spain. Argentinian Lionel Messi matches up against former Manchester United player Christiano Ronaldo – Ronaldo now makes his runs for Real Madrid, another Spanish club side. Ronaldo drives to the net and hits the cross-bar or post numerous times. The "shrinking" net of Real Madrid and the beautiful game of Barcelona prevail and, at the time, cast Messi and his national squad from Argentina in the role of frontrunners for the 2010 men's World Cup title in South Africa.[25] Messrs, Iniesta, Xavi, and Vila do have something else to say about that World Cup outcome for Spain and then after that for Barcelona again in the UEFA Cup championship in 2010.

Tournament cups and trophies like those in the World Cup are always on little kids' minds, and my Vipers are no exception with awards given out at the end-of-season team parties. These awards are presented to the players by Coach Stu and the parents. The parties that we throw for the children are awesome, and these trophies also provide me with great places to hide and hang out. Lurking around the festivities and unloosening shoelaces under the picnic tables are also some of my other hobbies.

Coach makes a point of choosing unique styles of trophies for the children. The league gives a trophy to all players at the end of the spring season. But for the fall, he feels the children deserve another trophy, and he searches through the catalogues for new ideas in trophies. He is likely to find something unusual for the kids, whether it is an acrylic bubble with a soccer player inscribed on it or a cleat and ball trophy. One year some dog tags are made that have the Viper logo embedded in them, and another year there are personal Viper T-shirts made up. At our nine-year reunion I am shocked at how many kids still have their Viper dog tags and T-shirts and show up with them. The children really look forward to these gifts that express our team pride.

These parties are great times for me and the kids. I always know that there will be hot chocolate in the fall, along with donuts and bagels. I know that I can mingle among all the guests and hide amidst the trophies or behind the hot chocolate dispenser. These soccer parties are unsurpassed for enduring friendships and happy times.

The Viper parties echo memories I have from the festive times growing up in the Amazon Rainforest. My family has also danced the night away in the Himalayas and Hung-San province in China, and we carry traditions by crossing the great seas to the Americas. The thundering hooves of the Mongol warriors dancing across the great steppes of China and Russia, the sound of clashing – metal as their swords meet – these are vivid memories imbedded in my monster mind through Poppa's stories. Couple these echoes with the Brazilian-Amazonian symphony and you arrive at pure joy. It creates a state of bliss and a feeling that I know touches the hearts of children throughout the history of the world like it does for these Vipers.

The next fall we have another exciting turn

of events. Koga is still kicking his cleats and laces off his feet as they will sometimes go flying high into the air. Every time one of those cleats launches into the air, it is a new record. We call it Viper aerial domination! The team has won five games, in this particular season with three of them each going by the score of 2–0. They also draw three times; the first game against the yelling coach and his team ending in a 0–0 tie. The second game, which is the most exciting game of this season, concludes as a thrilling come-from-behind 1–1 draw. The referees, who are high school players, come up to Coach Stu after the game to talk about how exciting a game it has been! Erich makes five or six clear saves, and keeps us hanging in the game.

The other team scores the game's first goal when Willy, one of our defenders, swings his leg and whiffs on a ball. He lands right on Erich's side. Now Willy's a big tough kid with curly blond hair and a full set of freckles, and when he lands on someone, that's gotta hurt! I don't know if the freckles weigh more than he does, but Will's a load. When I see him at the Viper reunion, he is still a big guy, only bigger, with the same great personality and smile. I watch and giggle as he just marches into the ice cream parlor, parks himself down, grabs a spoon, and proceeds to eat Coach Stu's ice cream sundae! I haven't seen the boy in nine years, but some things never change!

Back to the game because I get side-tracked. The other team jumps on the loose ball and score the initial goal. Erich is in pain from the injury to his side but keeps a quivering but stiff upper lip and resumes his place in the nets. Erich is also a tough kid. As a side note, his dad, Assistant Coach Bob, always asks Coach to recommend reading material for him since he is definitely not a reader. Coach recommends books such as the Corporal Chowderpants series, whose hero is performing daring deeds-of-do as long as he has some good old-fashioned New England "chowda" to eat. Hey, whatever stirs his soup or, more importantly, can get a kid to read, right?

Willy, or "Mad" Will as we call him, charges straight ahead at you like a rampaging bull. He has to learn that the offensive player can throw a fake and go around you when you make those defensive wild charges. One time, at practice, he accuses Erich of being "an animal, just an animal, and you should go play football instead of soccer!" I was surprised it wasn't time for another chicken reference. Willy says he is being fouled a lot by Erich, and Coach Stu has to calm him down. But on this particular game day, Will is playing well and the injury to Erich is caused by Will trying to clear a ball in the goal area and falling on Erich.

The tying goal comes when Renny dribbles through the entire defense on a breakaway and scores the goal for us with about two minutes left in the game. Delirium breaks loose in the stands and on the field! I am dancing my victory jig between blades of grass. Hip-hip, hop-hop, kick your heels up a lot, a lot! I give a personal interview to Monster News, telling all about how Will likes chicken nuggets. The saga of the soccer-playing chicken will live on after all!

CHAPTER 4:

THE SEASONS CONTINUE

Season five is going well for the Vipers soccer team. The team has a record of five wins, no losses, and three draws. The game of this week is phenomenal for a number of reasons. First, Coach Stu knows that the opposition is a disciplined and skilled team called "Blue Ice" and that they have a number of travel team players who are also playing in this recreational league. Their coach is big on yelling and chomping and puffing on cigars on the field (disgusting habits), and he knows several of the Vipers from coaching other sports in the past, particularly Jake from tee ball and baseball season. So Coach Stu knows ahead of time that this game will be a difficult one for his team. The other reason for a headache on this day is that seven or eight little Vipers misunderstand and think that the game is going to start later than at noon. They start showing up around 12:30. In particular, Cimmy is a West African child who can run like the wind and has always been an anchor of the team in midfield. His family is having problems and Cimmy cannot be counted on to show up for games at all.

With this backdrop of dilemmas surrounding the team and my constant tugging at Koga's laces, keeping them flipping and flapping around, the game starts. Coach Stu warns the Vipers of one player on the opposition who can hurt them with a big kick, and within minutes of the start of the game, sure enough, the Viper defense fails to clear a goal kick out of the defensive area, and that player kicks in a goal.

Everyone is so devastated, but they pick their heads up and, especially the defense, put a clamp on the opposition to prevent any other goals. Without Cimmy and Renny (one of our travel players who has a leg injury), the Vipers are left really shorthanded in the attacking third of the field.

Coach Stu repeatedly juggles the lineup, trying different combinations of players to see what could work. He finally seems to find the right mix. He puts Pico, the sole Mexican- American representative on the team, into the game. Pico, is a spinning, great dribbling player. On the right wing he positions big Chris and Ethan, who nails down the center forward position like he owns it. Coach does all this juggling while carrying on a "running" sideline dialogue with Jake, Alex, Joel, and Thomas. Those rascals are peeking into the donut boxes rather than watching the game.

The comical conversation goes something like this:

The Coach yells down the sideline, "What are you guys doing with the donuts?" Joel, speaking for the rest of his crew of donut hooligans or "dooligans," volunteers to speak up "We're just looking into what donuts were brought for after the game, Coach!" *That is a good one*, I think.

"Just looking at the donuts?"

The parents crack up when they hear that. It would be the first time some ten-year-olds are just "looking at the donuts!" We've got the video to prove this incident happened.

In the second half, this combination seems to jell (get it, "jell" – donuts, ha-ha). Gabe, who has been given a green light to bring the ball up from his sweeper position, advances the ball to big Chris. Now big Chris is usually a striker on the Vipers and is now being asked to play the right wing position. Who knew how well he would play? It is a chance we have to take being shorthanded.

I clearly remember that fateful day in the earlier part of the season when Coach decide to put him in the game; his laces are totally loose and tugged out by the king of swing and tug, yours truly.

Coach suspects a culprit was at work, and he instructs Chris to lace up before going in. Chris, for some reason, never ties up but rather goes straight to mom to say he can't get into the game. He eventually does get in the game, and his mom and Coach talk out issues after the game with mutual promises to stay on the laces problem and provide Chris with more time on the field.

Now, however, as the game rolls on it is the perfect time for big Chris to prove his courage, grab some glory. He sure comes through for all my little friends and teammates. He settles the ball and then slots it to Ethan. Ethan dribbles by several defenders and takes a shot. Big dude Chris, following up, is there for the tap-in and pokes it in for the tying score. Our fans are screaming in joy – these parents, brothers and sisters, dogs and pets, and, me. Forget about it, I am like a Mexican jumping bean jumping up and down and clapping my little hands while positioning myself on Koga's shoe tongue. I sway to the sounds again. I even add some *olé, olé's* to the cheer I am so excited. *Olé, olé, de joao, de joao, eh, eh, eh.* Coach Stu is so happy that the Vipers have tied this particular team. Parents say that the other coach's face is getting progressively bluer and redder. Believe it or not, the best and final chapter of this particular story has yet to be written and played out.

With probably five minutes left in the game, Ethan traps a loose ball to his feet and breaks free of the defense. For some reason, the other team's defenders have advanced up too far and leave a big gap in front of the goal. Ethan dribbles into that area, like the hero he is for the day and rockets in home free against the goalie – one-on-one. His shot sails into the right corner of the goal for the go-ahead goal! Pandemonium breaks loose! No one thought that this group of Vipers could beat the "Blue Ice," and with the clock running down, it now seems that the impossible was going to be achieved.

When the whistle blows to end the game, these children are so excited and happy; a better picture could not be painted. The boys lift Ethan way up in the air in a circle, and this is a snapshot for all time.

All our players and coaches stride out to give the traditional handshakes. The "Blue Ice" coach, however, makes matters worse for the kids by reluctantly shaking Coach Stu's hand. He begrudgingly offers it in response, but seems so annoyed that his team has lost. He is so ungracious that I just have to stick my tongue out at him. I also wiggle my ears which is another talent I have. I wiggle 'em fast like everything else that I do! I mean, come on, he's a grown man and that team's coach and he is supposed to set a positive example for his team.

The Viper children, even the little brothers and sisters, make a mad dash for the tunnel that the parents form. Ah yes, the tunnel. Parents and friends hold hands together and aloft in the sky while the children and I dash so happily through and under. This tunnel is a Viper tradition, win or lose, and that's important, win or lose! There are calls to do another tunnel at our reunion and of course, we have to recreate our scenes of glory one last time. It is also great when we see the teams in the eight-year-old game Coach Stu reffed a few weeks ago also enjoy a tunnel. Some things never change when kids are having fun!

Those alleged donuts and juice finally get eaten while the team's plans for the end-of-the-year party are discussed among the parents. They decide to hold it after the last game of the season. Ethan especially likes it when Coach Stu makes those little player introductions at the parties. One year, Coach Stu does not plan on making player speeches because of limited time at the party. Ethan keeps tugging on his shirt to remind him that he *must* do it and insists so much that the tradition of player intro's is carried on throughout the years. Coach Stu's wife still says she runs into grandparents of the kids who ask for the Coach and remember those player intros at the end of the seasons, and these are additional fond memories of Viper seasons. In this particular year, because of Ethan's tugging and insistence, Coach Stu does the now famous player intros and awards off the "dome" (that means he "wings" it, like the Soccer Chicken would have, ha-ha!). The team presents Coach

THE VIPER CAKE, TROPHIES & SWEATSHIRTS

Stu with a wonderful coach's sweatshirt that says his name and the year of the team. The boys each permanently sign the sweatshirt with their names. After the signings are done and the shirt studied, Coach Stu realizes that the shirt has been signed by the entire team and a mystery guest, "Seymour Butts" (a team joke). I want to sign the shirt also, but was way too busy stuffing Koga and Jay's laces into my puffy pouches! For me it is a gourmet dinner with music and dancing, and I just can't keep myself from tugging and sautéing those laces into a hearty meal!

CELEBRATE THE VICTORY OVER BLUE ICE

CHAPTER 5:

A SEASON NOT TO BE DENIED

The party is set to be held after the last game of the season. The Viper team is 6–0-3 and still glowing from the excitement of the recent stunning upset of the Blue Ice. This is most definitely an extremely happy team.

So who shows up to ref the last game? You guessed it: the Queen of Grinchdom, the Sultaness of Squelch. This game is against the orange team, and their defense is very stingy at giving up goals. Koga shows up late, and of course, within minutes of hitting the field, his laces have two feet to spare on them and are blowing in the wind.

"Hey, Koga, I love you!" I leap for joy over his socked feet and these loose laces, and the game goes on!

As usual, in a pressure game, no one wants to be the goalie; Larry conveniently claims his pinky still hurts from practice and insists he can't play goalie. Coach Stu appoints good old Matty to do the tending. Matty, uncharacteristically for him, is really nervous about being goalkeeper, but we score first on a fluke rebound. He gets uncharacteristically upset for him when we relinquish the lead and the other team scores to tie it up. You know how usually cool under fire Matty is. It really isn't his fault. Our whole defense is sagging and looking sluggish, and we also can't really generate any ball movement on offense.

The end of the first half finds Ethan being purposely tripped in the box. Our opposition is keying in on him. No call, naturally, by El Grincho. Coach Stu rarely screams on the sideline, but in this instance, he and Ethan let loose as they both scream so loud that dogs in the neighborhood start howling, but our protests fall on deaf ears. Wouldn't you know it, I am hiding behind that shrubbery and I see the whole play. We should be awarded a penalty kick that should have allowed us the opportunity to break the tie.

This same ref is also being a pain when it comes to allowing substitute patterns. She turns to coach, saying, *"No!"* in a most obnoxious way when he asks to be allowed for a substitution. It really seems like this ref has a real grudge against our team. Also, the Handy Dandy Monster Rule Book never taught me how to deal with mean referees, coaches and league commissioners. Maybe we are too happy as a team and she just can't handle seeing it.

Finally, at the beginning of the second half, Peter manages to tap a rebound into the goal area, and the ball trickles over the goal line. The other team yells that it isn't a goal, and we see the ref mulling the decision on the goal over and over as time ticks by. She finally calls the goal off. Good fortune finally shines on us though! The linesman is right there and insists on making the call. She is a middle school player with knowledge of the game rules. She tells the other coach and Ms. Grinchbottoms that the whole circumference of the ball has crossed the goal line and it does not matter where the goalie is positioned. That is the correct call and, I might add, one of the only fair ones my little team has ever gotten when she is working our games. We hang on to a 2–1 margin of victory. Spectacularly, it is the Vipers' first undefeated season. So sweet. 7-0-2, and fulfilling a five-year dream of Coach Stu and his boys.

The party that followed is, of course, sumptuous and includes a meal that most kids dream about. I have to confess that monsters dream about these parties also. The pizzeria down the street with the unbeatable prices on their pies delivers a dozen pies to the field. The Vipers always make a serious quest to find the greatest pizza pies. It is a goal of most little players I visit with. The best pies the Vipers find are in Brooklyn; thin sliced with the hot grease running off the pie. Guaranteed to burn the upper lid of your mouth. That's the test. Many Vipers from the past come back to visit with us. There are three trays of fudge brownies and a vanilla cake with the name *Vipers* drawn on the top in red icing.

There is also hot chocolate, coffee, and all kinds of juice. Coach Stu, naturally, has to make Ethan's favorite speeches and give out the Viper logo T-shirts.

The big event of the day is Jake; Erich; and, yes, a returning visitor, Mark (wearing a borrowed Viper shirt) leading the boys around the field with a Viper jersey on a stick. The stick and jersey become their flag-banner, and they climb up a tree trunk for a team picture. The boys and I vow to defend our fort from all attackers, especially the little girls, like Julia and Roxanne, Erich's sisters. They call it Fort Viper, and it becomes an historic landmark in local soccer lore. Now every time we pass the stump, we always say, "Remember Fort Viper," instead of "Remember the Alamo" and its heroes who died in the battle, such as Davey Crockett and Jim Bowie – the Indian fighter in the War for Texas Independence.[25]

I even make a grass crown for my teeny-tiny head and have on an eye patch to make me look like a pirate. The sounds, music, and beat of the kids' soccer world have reached another high point in our fifth season together.

REMEMBER VIPER MOUNTAIN

CHAPTER 6:

THE WINTER INDOOR SOCCER SEASON OR "HOW I SURVIVE THE SNOW AND LEARN TO DRIBBLE IN SMALL SPACE"

Every winter, the soccer players in colder regions of the United States face a dilemma. Because of the weather, many indoor soccer facilities have sprung up using artificial grass turf or gym floors. They are primarily geared to keeping a child's foot on the ball and teaching him or her how to dribble in "small space."

Coach Stu also coaches a winter league for some of his Vipers, which is in a gym and uses a Nerf-like ball that is played off the gym walls. The boys enjoy that type of "wall-ball." They call their team either the Yellow or Green Forest Dragons, depending on the jersey color.

One year Jake's kick from midfield is the winning goal in the playoff championship. Jake says he doesn't like to talk about it because of all the congratulations heaped upon him. Jake's perspective is that he classifies himself as a defender and that he is not supposed to score.

Coach Stu; Jake's brother, Jase; their mom; and I are all in attendance for that kick (in our minds it *replays in s-l–o-w m-o-t-i-o-n* because we want to keep savoring the moment), and we always mention it to the Jakester with heaps of great praise.

In the indoor season, we are again, plagued by Empress Sourball – the Grinchess Referee who shows up again and again to torment these poor little players. The team the Dragons are playing is the one with three travel team players on it, and two of them are from the U-11 State Cup second place team. They should not be allowed to play on the same team in this recreational league since it is an unfair advantage for them. It seems like the Big Commish always sets the teams up that way. These boys can kick real hard, and despite this, the little Dragons of recreational players and one B-team travel player are, miraculously ahead in the second half by the amazing score of 4–3. It is exciting, and then the situation deteriorates.

The other team, in attempting to dominate, starts pushing kids and kicking dangerously. The referee lets the game get out of control. Coach Stu protests to her, in what becomes an all-to-familiar act and ask for explanations of some of her no-calls.

The next thing the referee says is, "I don't like people up in my face like you, and this game is called off!" And she walks out of the gym, leaving all the people in the stands and on the sidelines shocked.

Fortunately for the Vipers another older student is enlisted to referee the second half and does a good job with no further incidents. The Green Forest Dragons lose, but the game is exciting and peacefully concludes. No complaints.

Another game in the tournament between these teams has further incidents with this referee. After the other team scores, she shockingly gives possession to the same team.

When our players call it to her attention, she says, "It doesn't matter! Don't worry about it!" It is as if she doesn't care about the rules and just wants the other team to dominate us.

The boys come running to Coach to complain. He complains once again to the ref and gets no reaction. These complaints should cause her, at minimum, to be reprimanded by the Big Commish, if not being relieved of her refereeing duties.

On the lighter side, one child on another tournament team keeps kicking his sneakers off into the air every game, pie à la Koga, and kids are ducking left and right to avoid being hit. One of the parents yells out from the stands, "Hey, ref! Tell that kid to tie up his sneakers! He almost hit my kid in the head!"

I have to chuckle because I am sure doing my job. Oh, by the way, the Dragons finish the tournament in third place – not bad!

At another indoor tournament, this referee disallows a goal for our team that would probably put us in the championship game. The ball clearly crosses the goal line, with its entire circumference over the line and in the net. This same type of situation happened in the outdoor season, remember?

We always hope there will be no further interactions like this between the children,

Coach Stu, parents, and this referee. And you know what? Despite all the children's difficulties with this referee, they enjoy playing in the gym on those cold winter days, and that makes the experiences worthwhile for them.

Needless to say, I enjoy these winter seasons in different ways from the outdoor campaigns. I get a chance to snuggle with all that soccer equipment during the winter. I am happiest when I can find a fresh-cut pine tree log and build a home inside of it for the holiday season.

CHAPTER 7:

PANCAKES:
THE BREAKFAST OF MONSTERS
AND CHAMPIONS

I already told you that Jase is Jake's brother. Would you believe he can eat pancakes before every game he plays in? Pancakes have always been his favorite food, smeared with maple syrup, and he even dunks strips of crispy bacon into extra gobs of syrup.

He says pancakes give him the winning edge, and who are we to doubt him? He hit the speed gun with his kicks at forty-nine miles per hour when he was eleven years old. His travel soccer team also has won three consecutive State Cup titles and a Regional Snickers Championship.

Jase in one game has his kick hit the crossbar from mid-field and bounce out. The response from some of the old Prospect Unity Club members was that " they did that and also put the ball into the back of the net" You can never beat the old-timers!

The other thirteen boys on his team are also filled with glee and merriment at having won the state championships. As a side note, why do ten-to-thirteen-year-olds usually go into restaurant bathrooms and start a ruckus with the soap? What is that about? Are they attracted to soap machines, the colors of the liquid soap, and truly enjoy making a mess? We don't know, but it's an age-old question. Coach Stu and his wife don't recall ever having their own childhood penchant for bathroom destruction. But Jake says he remembers at one birthday party at the movie theater that he and his friends were running out from the bathroom with a roll of toilet paper trailing behind them!

As to goofiness, Jase is no different than his brother and his friends. One time I recall he locked the bathroom door in the restaurant from the outside before shutting the door. Coach Stu had to use the bathroom after that and found it locked. He still, to this day, suspects that this was Jase's handiwork, and rightly so.

During the winter holiday vacation, Jase is riding in the car with his gloves sticking out from under his wool beanie like moose antlers and he is yelling out the window at passersby the immortal question, "Do you like baloney?" Coach Stu says, "he's going to either cut him out of his will or put him up for adoption", and Jase asks, "Can you do that?" Coach thinks Jase gets a little nervous when he threatens to do that.

Jase always has these two evil, demonic laughs when he pulls one of his pranks. These laughs are either a sort of a squeaky sound or a horse's whinny.

We all remember what happens at one of the state championship tournaments. We stop at the local truck stop near the fields. The boys are only in the store for a few minutes prior to the game, and Jase and Jake are looking at different items in the store. Out of the corner of his eye, Coach sees a display rack of holiday toy trucks tottering back and forth dangerously. The next thing he spots is the line of boxes falling over and two young kids and a wisp of smoke, namely me, scurrying out of the store on the other side. How Jase and Jake ever get out of there without the manager catching them is beyond Coach Stu's grasp. He reprimands them about these antics, but somehow, when the temptation presents itself, whoops, here it goes again!

JASE PLAYS TRAVEL SOCCER

Listen to this story! On Jase's team, KiKi definitely loses his mind when he moons his teammates and other customers coming into a local Dippy's restaurant, and from the large front window of the restaurant no less! The team is at one of its out-of-state tournaments. Things get a little bit carried away because Kiki's parents, who own their own airplane, are flying somewhere on business. Maybe they should fly less and watch their child more. They leave KiKi under another parent's care while they have this business meeting. I mean for sure "Seymour Butts" pays us another visit that day.

What makes kids do these crazy things in public places? Is it a plague that haunts parents? Is it some diabolical curse that a monster like me has placed on the children? Couldn't kids just tone it down a wee bit so we all might live in peace for a change? Not!

Despite the momentary loss of sanity, these are the original team members who founded their club, and they are also, just like the Vipers, an exceptionally friendly and tight-knit team unit. Five of these players do go on to collegiate careers in Division I soccer.

THE CHOPPY

Coach Stu, is, on this trip, wearing his parent hat and helping to barbecue when there is an important game or tournament coming up. Parent involvement helps continue the winning tradition. At one tournament in Maryland, we actually buy crabs and clams on the road and cook them at the hotel. The team families are about seventy-five percent Portuguese, and they know how to season the food since they love seafood.

Now when I cook, on the other hand, I will always mix various fruit and veggies with some fancy laces, a lot of passion and excitement, and grass blades; put them in my mini blender; and make what I call a "Choppy." This is a lumpy, bumpy drink that is only for Monsters. Monsters need a nutritious, balanced diet also, just like kids.

Kids, please don't eat boot laces and grass blades like monsters do. Stick to your fruit and veggies coupled with passion, excitement, and energy. It's much better for your health!

Whatever team I am with at a particular time, I am prepared to see these boys go through their soccer careers. For me, I can mingle with town league teams of happy youngsters on the fields of

BRICKLES SOCCER ACADEMY BUS RIDE

a small town or at schoolyards. I can also change environments and switch to these green-bladed grass fields of the elite travel teams. For me, the most important thing is the energy of the children that keep smiles on all our faces.

CHAPTER 8:

THE BRICKIES SOCCER ACADEMY

Now I will tell you about my newest experiences with what the kids call "Da Brickies." Coach Stu misses coaching. So recently, he got back in it again, coaching and training young people. He brings a bunch of underprivileged city kids to a free indoor clinic at the Brickies Soccer Academy.

"Hitting the Bricks" or "Da Brickies" – a beautiful turf field setting that many of these kids cannot afford to attend normally. These kids range in ages from eight to seventeen and have a variety of skill sets. He is working with the eight and nine-year-old boys particularly mixed in with some of the teenage girls from Coach's high school team, Team Revolt. I go along for the ride and find some new kids to cling to.

"Flashing" Dervin, the eight-year-old Guatemalan child with the great soccer feet, times his jumps over would-be tacklers and has great vision on the field. The kids call him the little Messi because he always wears his Barcelona jersey. And let me tell you I yank his shoelaces loose countless times and that kid just keeps flashing those moves. What a marvel! Choo-Choo is an aggressive eight-year-old child with a nose for the goal. His buddy Coco, who is a bit older and competitive, wants to win no matter the cost, and he will slide tackle on the turf rug to prove it. And the girls, oh my goodness, they are great! These high schoolers are happy to be there twice a week playing with some other high school girls from their league but other school programs, as well as the younger boys. They all are learning while playing, and that is the important thing. Other coaches like "Laughing" Harris and "Dancing" Pete add to the camaraderie with Coach Stu.

Also, they are learning lessons in life skills, like how to behave while using the facilities. For instance, some pretzels and chips go missing — "grew legs" from the canteen. We hold a group meeting, and Coach puts down the law that all the kids have to ante up at the next practice and bring a couple of dollars and put it in the pot to replace the stolen snacks. No questions are asked, no accusations made, and no prisoners taken – the money is returned by all players. Lesson learned.

There are also some top-level high school male African players from Liberia playing in these practices. This mixture of young and old all travel on the bus under Coach Stu's tutelage. The bus ride raps are cool. This one's called "Scholar or Thug:"

Hey, suckkah, no more bread and buttah.
You'd better always listen to your muddah.

And ask yourself the question:

Scholar or thug?

You're looking like a mug Going to classes

With wave cap and granny glasses,
*   in the inner city,*

It's really not too pretty;

Pressure being put amidst the concrete soot.
Take your book bag,

Stash it or walk the streets
*   looking like a geek?*

Gotta make a choice.
Listen up you got an inner voice

Telling you the future is
*   where you want to get to.*

So make a decision
*   amidst the hood's derision:*

Composition,
*   Mathematician, Hydrogen,*

And that's called Education.

Duck the Bullet,
Bite the Bullet,

Sink your teeth into it.

A book's not for show;
only a map to help you get go.

So listen to your teacher
*   and your coach.*

They're only trying to reach ya.

Gotta grab the hand
*   before hourglass loses all sand.*

I like the bus rides down and back to the high school. The rides are full of noise, chatter, and arguments. "Pure energy." Sometimes empty juice bottles go shizzing and whizzing through the air. Coach Stu gets that issue settled very quickly. Lots of skills on the field, songs on the bus, and more lessons to be learned. Who is a better team: Arsenal, Barcelona, PSG, Real Madrid, Juventus or Chelsea? I don't think there is any doubt now about Real Madrid's ranking as number one at the present time but if PSG and Neymar, Alves and Mbappe have anything to say on it that may change.[26]

Donny sneaks girl on the bus.

On a historical note, how good is George Manneh Weah as the best footballer to come out of Africa and his native Liberia? He is the FIFA footballer of the year for 1995, three-time African player of the year, and has even run for President of his country in 2004 and now stands on the threshold of winning the contest to be installed as the country's next President. He graduated as an honor student from DeVry Institute of Miami, Florida – a goal he never thought he would achieve. He is also an international ambassador for peace.[27] George Weah certainly sets the standard for all kids to follow. So of course, arguments and history lessons continue on the Brickies bus rides all the way back home.

The staff and high school players have also formed a new team, The Danger Zone, for state tournaments on the weekends. Sometimes the Academy provides a beat-up, old van with bald tires, which Coach reluctantly drives. The van has a "mere" 167,000 miles on it. Like I said, the noise level in those buses or vans is ear splitting. Usually a few of the team's girlfriends join the team in the van. The van-o-meter says seventeen people can fit pretty comfortably. The type of music being played by Donny on the CD playerUsually a few of the team's girlfriends join the team in the van. The van- o-meter says seventeen people can fit pretty comfortably. The type of music being played by Donny on the CD player is pretty cool. I also like the team vibes because these are very positive kids. These guys range in age from fourteen to sixteen years old, so a lot of the conversations in the bus are about girls and music, of course. What else is there at that age but sports, girls, and music? Donny is a team culprit. Someone says they spot him behind a bush giving his girlfriend a kiss. That is a story that carries over from last season, but now, as we understand it, they have broken up. It should be interesting to hear about the new adventures of Donny and Company.

Coach Stu likes to give out nicknames to team members. He names the twins Shaz and Baz; each wears their baseball caps in different ways, and that is the only way you can tell them apart. They are street-ball experts on the soccer pitch and the possessors of a bagful of one-on-one moves. The twins, however, are not good at following instructions, and they like to free-lance. This brings back memories of Daniel on the Vipers. In fact, after six weeks of training, the twins are still freelancing and not running the set plays and defensive formations Coach has designed. So Coach chooses to utilize their special abilities at coming off the sideline to light scoring fires under the team when needed, and they sure can score goals! The twins also store corny jokes on their handheld computers, which they tell at every opportunity. Give us a break, guys!

There is also the kid nicknamed Fletch, who is just plain nervous in the games. He has good dribbling skills, which Coach thinks are the number-one priority skill in the game. Fletch plays much better when he is calm and stress free, but the trick is getting him to reach that point. Coach says the more game situations you are in as a player, the calmer you will be as the pressure mounts, and I tend to agree with that. "Playing cold" is the expression being used these days to describe this situation. One memorable event when the team really does "play cold" is when the team gets stuck in the van in a huge snowstorm after a Sunday afternoon game. Coach manages to get that bucket of nuts and bolts up three of the huge hills on the mountain, but the last one proves to be too much. The older boys jump out of the van to push lots of cars similarly stuck up the mountain. They even find a wallet with credit cards and money in the snow, along with keys, and bring this stuff to Coach Stu. The boys save many motorists with smiles on their faces, and they themselves don't even know when and how *they* will be getting off the mountain. That's the kind of kids they are. Many of them also show up unannounced for the funeral when Jase and Jake's grandfather passes away. I am proud as a monster to call the Brickies' team members my friends.

CHAPTER 9:

WHERE ARE THE SOCCER HEROES OF THE PAST?

Many of these little kids have fathers, grandfathers, or friends whose families play soccer. We know the names of the soccer heroes from years gone by. That's how we learn about all the legendary stars who have played this game of soccer. This is also how kids decide to pick their uniform numbers. Every little kid will like to wear a number from some famous soccer star. Kids can't help it; they want to be like those cleat commercials in the World Cup and Champions League. So uniform number and color selection are a big part of youth soccer.

With the turn of the twentieth century and the advent of modern soccer in Brazil, the name of Arthur Friedenreich probably does not spring to mind, but listen, kids, make no mistake about it; he is a legend of the game. He is known as "*El Tigre*," the Tiger. He has a German father and a black Brazilian mother. Slight in nature, he is quick to pounce on loose balls and follow them up into the goal. Believe it or not, he plays in his era over a twenty-six-year career. He plays in the 1920s with Vasco da Gama at the Rio de Janeiro club. He scores over 1,300 goals.[28] His luster as a goal scorer is only surpassed by the exploits of Pele in the 1950s and 1960s for the Santos Club in Brazil.[29] Few people know about this master of goal scoring because they begin their soccer life with the name of his successor, Pele, etched into their soccer memories.

Other stars have brought their skills to the Brazilian soccer scene. Garrincha plays in the same era as Pele and possesses superb dribbling skills despite having been born with a deformity to his leg.[30] Dunga, in the men's World Cup of 1998, plays with his spiky hair and ice-cold demeanor, which shows his determination to keep all attackers away from the goal.

His real name is Carlos Bledom Verri. He is the 2010 men's World Cup Brazilian national team coach and brings his steely determination to the team in a new, controlled style of play[31] while Carlos Alberto in the Pele era is such a smooth defender, hard to move out of your path with the ball.[32] Both of these defenders are team captains. In the 2002 men's World Cup, we bear witness to Rivaldo, Ronaldinho, and Ronaldo – the heroes of the day – scoring goal after goal for Brazil.[33] Other great players pass through our collective memories from different cultures of Europe. These players, in their own way, demonstrate the same type of creative inspiration on the soccer field. Gordon Banks, the one-eyed British keeper, is famous for making what is probably renowned as the most famous save against Pele in the 1970 men's World Cup.[34] Imagine playing the game with just one working eye, the result of a car accident and subsequent loss of vision and depth perception. Lev Yalcin, the unflappable Soviet goalie, the "Black Panther" always wears black, like a B-movie western action or superhero bringing his acrobatics to the goal.[35] The memories of these players always bring a smile to my face. Those are the game masters.

Offensively, George Best of the English Manchester United Club is known for juggling a ball right down the field. As a young boy in England he learns to dribble a tennis ball for countless hours. He is a bright meteor on the soccer scene that comes and leaves in a career of only five superstar years.[36] Johann Cruyff is the star of the Dutch club, Ajax, and inventor of a playing style of "total soccer." He also develops the "Cruyff," or "open gate" move of dribbling deception.[37]

Defensively, as well as with the ball, Franz Beckenbauer is given high esteem for inventing the offensive sweeper position for the West German national team and the Bayern-Munich Club in the late '60s and 1970s. What I always remember is the way he just glides fast when he has to. I call it conservation of energy. He is known as "The Kaiser" for orchestrating the field of play, and his ultimate moment is when he bursts past a defender.[38] His teammate on the New York Cosmos of the North American Soccer League is Giorgio Chinaglia. Giorgio is a physical striker who sets the record for the most goals scored in that league. He is lethal in turning and shooting with a quick release of the ball.[39] We lost Giorgio recently but his legacy lives on.

Charles Stillitano one of the hosts of the Soccer Show on BeIn Sports quotes Chinaglia as saying " that the problem with today's stars is they put on the gel, cologne and mousse before the game and that the stars of yesteryear put it on after the game.[40] I think that description fits in this age of TV commercials like Christiano Ronaldo being locked out of his hotel room in his underwear and his Instagram dilemma.[41]

It is this varied mix of styles in the game of soccer that creates excitement for the fans of the great French and Argentina teams. The respective team stars, Zenedine Zidane[42] and Gabriel Batistuta[43] play in more flexible styles depending on what the opposition is throwing at them in the way of defensive strategies.

We really enjoy the 2010 men's World Cup in South Africa and the emergence of the American squad with newcomers like Josey Altidore and Johnny Davis coupled with the likes of experienced Landon Donovan.[44]

The South Korean team is being touted as an upset maker. The Korean team bears the legacy of the 1966 "Red Mosquito" team of North Korea, which is the only Korean team to advance in World Cup play, defeating the Italian team that year. They next go ahead of Portugal 3–0 in the quarterfinals, only to have Eusebio, another great name from the past, score four goals in thirty-two minutes and lose 5–3. That team goes home to disgrace in North Korea. The communist regime claims they have been ill prepared for this quarterfinal match, having partied too much after the Italian victory. All but one of the players, allegedly, are sentenced to twenty years in an internment camp, and only in 2002 are the players brought out to receive medals from the government, honoring their great victory – just an amazing story in the backdrop of the 2002 Korean/Japanese-hosted men's World Cup.[45]

I look forward to the long-awaited emergence of the American game from its hibernation. Heck, it takes forty years for the Americans to make it to the men's World Cup again after their 1950 victory over England. I hope you remember that rag-tag team of immigrants who band together in Brazil to put a 'hurtin' on the big bad British team of Sir Stanley Matthews. The score stands at 1–0. The game winner is by one Joe Gaetjens, a Haitian who history has sort of gobbled up and made disappear in the aftermath of Haitian dictator, Francois Duvalier, "Poppa Doc." No one has heard from him since the team's moment in the sun. This team of rank amateurs is greeted upon their arrival back at the airport by one lonesome and solitary fan back home in the U. S, and that is player Walter Bahr's wife.[46]

No, the game in America is certainly changing and with the little ones training under my tutelage it will continue to improve and bring America closer to the level of the world's game. I am looking forward to maybe bringing these kids to a state of readiness in achieving World Cup status for the men's world cup of 2022 in Qatar. After all, I learn my lessons well at the Eenie-Meenie-Miney-Mo school on Gobbledy Guck Lane, and the passion I have for the game I have brought to the Vipers, Team Revolt and 'Da Brickies' and will continue to give to my own young students here in America.

The 2014 men's World Cup returns home to Brazil, where it all began for this Shoelace Monster. I think at the time that the hiring of Jürgen Klinsmann on August 1, 2011, as head soccer coach of the U.S. men's national team, creates a style for the team reflecting the mix of cultures in the United States. The points Jürgen makes are well taken about the college game in this country. The college game, in many instances, is a chaotic, wide-open style of "long ball," and training is only for three months a year. There is a need for technical skill on the ball that requires longer training and seeing the field at 180-degree angles or with greater vision.[47]

Now we know that Jürgen's vision remains unrealized with his firing 5 years later. Bruce Arena takes over the U.S. Men's National Team but fails to get the U.S. into the 2018 World Cup. We refer all readers to the *"Soccer Tales Coloring Book – Reset of U.S. Soccer"* and the time line for the men's team culminating in their October 10, 2017 loss to Trinidad and elimination from the World Cup qualifiers.[48]

Remember kids, just like with Fletch on the Brickies, it is imperative to remain calm in soccer as the passion of the game unfolds and surrounds you. This is something that is being sought in American soccer and this monster, for one, is looking for a big upgrade in the American game with a change in the Men's team coaching, along with the February 10, 2018, election of Carlos Cordeiro to the presidency of the USSF steward-ship. More to follow in the Postscript.

I look forward to the emergence of the American game. Similarly, true to my roots, I admire the Brazilian style of soccer and know its place in history. I can still hear those musical rhythms that sing out to me at home. My hopes and dreams are that in one of the remote villages, another little child will hear the sounds and dance rhythms of the magical instruments of the *pandeiro* and *reco-reco*,[49] the drum pattern called *Baiao*, the dance rhythms known as *Xaxado* from the Northeast African influence on Brazil, and the *Ijexa*[50] that drift in to be carried by native musicians as far away as to the big city of Rio De Janeiro. *De joao, de joao, eh, eh, eh!*

I also have a northern echo in my ear as Iceland qualifies for the 2018 World Cup for the first time in history. They are the smallest nation, with 330,00 residents, to ever qualify.

Ironically, the smallest nation previous to them is Trinidad and Tobago. It's a generation of players coming through in Iceland that have been together a long time and there's a rumor that there are still more to come.

People say there's a unity in the team. They seem to love playing for each other, with each other just like my Vipers.

Listen to the drums of the Icelanders as they cheer their team on. This passion is what our

U.S. National team should be all about. We will have to find our way to it.

In American youth soccer culture, we should try to teach some of these different styles to our children and make up street soccer games, popular for our own country. Little friendly competitions between the children on the soccer fields, picking their countries of choice and reviving these stars of the past, will continue to add to the growth and popularity of the game. Appearances by popular players like David Beckham on the James Corden TV show and his play for the MLS team, Los Angeles Galaxy,[51] also help fuel the popularity of the sport. These little street games also bring back fond memories for me of the great players who are friends of mine as I travel throughout the world.

CHAPTER 10:

RUMINATIONS, LAMENTATIONS, AND FONDEST OF MEMORIES

All of these stories are part of this monster's recollections from my stay in the United States. I fondly recall all the friends that have been made and the wonderful cleats and shoelaces that I have become attached to. I now know how wonderful the playing fields and training facilities in America are for the players. I really feel that if America puts her mind to developing the necessary esprit for soccer, the sport will become as popular here as it is all over the world. The men's World Cup in 2002, when they reach the quarter-finals, is proof of how well America can do.[52] I think we have to capture more of the joy of playing. Jake's brother, Jase, plays a tournament as a twelve-year-old for his travel team. He has the opportunity to play against Mexico's Giovanni Dos Santos. "Gio" is equally brilliant as a twelve-year-old, filled with enthusiasm for this game of soccer. We see that great smile and happiness on display at the 2011 Gold Cup final against the United States and in leading Mexico to first place in the CONCACAF qualifying tournament for this year's World Cup. In the span of a few minutes in the second half, he manufactures one of the greatest highlight reel goals of all time. I will freeze the smile on his face for posterity. He leads Mexico to these titles. This monster thinks America is capable of producing the same smiles of joy in the future as they win on the world stage.[53] America develops its young player pool, but at the same time, we need to cultivate even more kids who appreciate and experience the joy and passion of the world's beautiful game.

This monster is concerned when he reads news headlines about overbearing parents. I am alarmed at incidents of parents intervening with coaches over playing time issues or soccer woes on whether a child makes a specific travel team.[54]

I recall the conversations I overhear from the substitute players on that Mexican U-12 team. They only live and concentrate on soccer in their lives. They say they do not pay attention to school. The question then is, what of their future after their playing days are over? On the flip side of the debate, there are those who think America is coddling its children too much in rewarding athletic mediocrity.[55]

The Honduran men's national team coach is quoted as saying that "American kids get iPads® for Christmas presents while Honduran kids receive soccer balls."[56]

I think the Vipers are an example of how a group of not particularly high-level skilled children can, over a five-year period, vastly improve their skills, learn teamwork and cooperation with each other, and build a joy of the game that will last them a lifetime. *There, I've made my serious speech!*

Now this little guy is looking forward to the next season, when the spring sunshine warms the air and the grass tops grow green again. For it is then that I will hear, once more, the familiar sounds of boot meeting ball, happiness, and squeals of delight and flowing jokes and pranks that come from the young people playing the game I love.

I know I only have a few years to work with these little ones. Within a few years, many of my former victims can double tie their laces real tight and make their mark in the world. The victims will now be the victors.

Hark, me thinks I hear a new group of toddlers waiting on the practice fields of the Kiddy-kickers. For this moment I again hear the native song of rhythm beginning with a drumbeat and the echoing bang of a branch beating on a carved-out log. I usher in a new season and new beginnings. *De joao, de joao, eh, eh, eh!*

EPILOGUE

And so it comes to pass that the Vipers meet again nine years later and for one last time. Coach Stu sends out emails and goes on the Internet network for the invites. Many of the boys heed the call, and out they come: Erich, Mad Will, Mark, Jake, Jase, and James – to name a few. These boys are on the eve of going to college, and yet it seems that time is frozen for the Vipers. The reunion shows, nine years later, the positive feelings they have for their Viper experiences. Their stories continue to amaze me. Koga is now a shoe salesman at a large department store, *"Shoe Dreams,"* tying up laces for customers. Matty is a waiter at the hottest restaurant in town, specializing in – what else? – ice cream sodas. Jase has gone on to play soccer for a Division I university. Will is planning to act on stage as he has done throughout high school and and also to begin engineering school. James is thinking of taking a year off to contemplate the world and then continue on to college. Erich is thinking of becoming an elementary school teacher (ironically, teaching little kids to read). Julia, Erich's sister, is playing travel team soccer. Mark, Julio, and Ethan write back many times to apologize for being away on vacation and having to miss the reunion. Ethan sends at least 150 pictures of his entire wrestling career. Jake is considering a career in archaeology, having traveled to Kenya this past summer. He also hosts a college radio show. Coach Stu continues to referee youth soccer matches and coach high school soccer. We do the tunnel one last time in the restaurant as the waitresses laugh and giggle along with us.

This restaurant/ice cream parlor is where they filmed the last episode of a TV gangster show. Amazingly, a busload of Brits come through on tour, looking for America, and boy do we give them a show! We, in turn, have a chance to talk British soccer with them.

The world just seems right.

AFTERWORD

We also anticipate a great men's World Cup final in South Africa in 2010 and are not disappointed. Coach Stu is in Tokyo, Japan, emailing us about the match. He and some other American coaches watch the match on Japanese television at 3:30 a.m. Mr. Iniesta and his teammates from the Spanish side work hard to score that lone goal and make it stand up for the victory. These players double their claim to fame while playing for Barcelona. This Spanish League team can rightfully put itself at or near the top of the list as one of the great club teams for the ages.[57] The women of the United States are equally involved as the World Cup plays out in Germany in the summers of 2011 and 2015 with the initial loss to Japan in the final. We applaud the United States women's team for their valiant effort in taking second place. In 2011, we usher in a new group of players to the U.S. Women's National team. Still being led by the old guard of more experienced players like Abby Wambagh, we have the addition of players like the gorgeous Hope Solo, fashion and dance model, and Alex Morgan, the girl that every little monster and boy falls in love with. There are also a cast of other wonderful players. Obviously, you can be cute and still have tremendous athleticism and soccer skills. My favorite player is Megan Rapinoe. She is always a classic scrapper, fighting with abandon and passion for every loose ball on the field. The United States loses in the finals against Japan on the heels of their epic victories over Brazil and France. Despite the flash, dash, and magic on the ball displayed by my home girls from Brazil, Marta, Christiane, and Fabiana, those girls are defeated by the stamina and come-back-ability (that's right; it's a new word to add to our soccer dictionary) the U.S. team display.[58]

Take, for example, Abby's goal against France in the semifinals. This is typical of the team's grit. She says, "I said head on ball, ball in goal."[59]

Abby and her teammates do their best in the heartfelt loss to Japan in the finals. I have to give all the credit in the world to the Japanese girls. They swarm to the ball whenever possible and help preserve pride for a country wracked by the March 2011 twin disasters of the earthquake and tsunami. Best of luck, Japan, in rebuilding your country. From what I understand, several of the ladies lost friends in the disaster. Before every game, the team rolls out a banner that reads, "To our Friends Around the World – Thank You for Your Support."[60] They deserve all the hurrahs. Be proud of your country in winning its first women's World Cup,

We certainly haven't forgotten the great U.S. women's run to the 1999 women's World Cup title against China with the likes of golden girls Mia Hamm; Judy Foudy; Kristine Lilly; goalie, Briana Scurry; and Brandi Chastain.[61]

I rekindle my faith in Women's World Cup soccer with the 2015 championship win redeeming themselves against Japan riding the strong leg of Carli Lloyd and her mates. The summary of those proceedings is captured in the annals *of Soccer Tales III-Baba Yaga's Revenge.*[62]

Now I "holla" to the world, watch out, the U.S. Men's national team is coming back for 2022 in Qatar. My mantra will always be amidst the musical refrains and drumbeats as "soccer does make the world go round." Indeed.

ENDNOTES

1. http://www.brazilproductions.com/html/ instrument.html

2. http://www.soccer-training-info.com/ ginga_nike_soccer.asp

3. *ESPN the Magazine*, November 4, 2017, p.12 story by Bruce Schoenfeld

4. http://www.fifa.com/worldcup/matches/ round=255959/match=300186501/index.html

5. http://www.bluker.com/rtbrazil/space.html

6. Ibid., http://www.soccer-training-info.com/ ginga_nike_soccer.asp

7. https://en.wikipedia.org/wiki/2002_FIFA_ World_Cup_Final

8. http://www.linguateca.pt/GikiCLEF/GIRA/ pool/GikiCLEF2009DocumentPool/en/b/r/a/ Brazil_national_football_team.html

9. https://www.quora.com/Why-do-some-players- wear-two-different-colored-football-boots-in- the-2014-World-Cup

10. https://www.footballboots.co.uk/history.html

11. Ibid.

12. http://www.rovers.co.uk/ club/view/history_list

13. http://fifaworldcup.yahoo.com/ com/en/pf/h/cp/ bra/pele.html

14. www.cits.net/china-travel-guide/cuju-the-fore-runner-of-modern-soccer.html

15. http://www.aztec-history.com/ancient-az-tec-games.html

16. Op.cit. http://www.rovers.co.uk/club/view/ history_list

17. https://en.wikipedia.org/wiki/Brad_Friedel

18. http://www.usafutsal.com/forms/ morefutsal. htma450275/history#histo

19. http://www.travelnotes.org/Football/2002/ Korea-Japan/Teams/D

20. https://www.quora.com/Why-did-Zidane-lose-his-cool-in-the-2006-World-Cup-finals

21. http://www.chron.com/sports/dynamo/ article/Italy-s-Cannavaro-wins-Gold-en-Ball-1878086.php

22. http://www.planetworldcup.com/CUPS/ 1998/wc98story.html

23. https://www.youtube.com/watch?v= SHOkhX_fdmQ

24. http://fifaworldcup.yahoo.com/en/020618

25. http://www.cyberpatriot.com/newspaper/ Alamo.html

26. *ESPN the Magazine*, Nov. 4, 2017, Op.Cit.

27. https://www.bloomberg.com/news/articles/
2018-01-22/ex-soccer-star-george-weah-to-take-
office-as-liberia-s-president

28. https://thesefootballtimes.com/2016/11/18/
remembering-arthur-friedenrich-brazils-
first-superstar/

29. Op.cit. http:fifaworldcup.yahoo. com/
com/en/pf/h/cp/bra/pele.html

30. http://www.worldcuparchive.com/
LEGENDS/garrincha.html

31. http://www.geocities.com/colosseum/
Midfield/1357/dunga.html

32. http://www.fifa.com/classicfootball

33. http://www.fifa.com/worldcup/
archive/edition=4395/overview.html

34. http://www.geocities.com/colosseum/
Field/3163/banks.html

35. http://quark./u.sc/oxama/lev

36. http://georgebestofficial

37. http://www.ynw62.dial.pipex.com/cruyff.htm

38. www.terra.com/specials/sports.cons/
beckenbauer_en.html

39. http://www.imdb.com/name/nm1705020/

40. https://www.rotowire.com/soccer/
showArticle.htm?id=17915

41. https://www.youtube.com/watch?v=
XTVXufBRN14

42. http://www.zidaneweb.com

43. http://www.wsoccer./om/players/batistuta

44. http://www.ussoccer.com/teams/mens/index.jsp.html

45. http://www.fifaworldcup.yahoo.com/en/pf/h/pwc/1966.html "Koreans:1966 Champions on Home Soil."

46. www.nytimes.com/2009/12/10/sports/soccer/10soccer.html?pagewanted=all

47. http://www.ussoccer.com/Multimedia/Media-Center.aspx#/id=0dfd468e-1e8b-4525–8d9f-9b37967bdd28

48. http://www.brazilproductions.com/html/instrument.html

49/50. http://sambaolywa.org/whatissamba.htm#

51. https://youtube.com/watch?v=l_0KtxzKZMw

52. Op.cit. http://www.fifaworldcup.yahoo.com

53. http://espngo.com/blog/los-angeles/soccer/post/-/id/9173-on- mexico-beats-u-s-in-gold-cup-final

54. http://www.nays.org/fullstory.cfm?articleid=10573

55. http://www.azcentral.com/families/articles/0302fam_overindulge.html

56. *Soccer Tales Coloring Book – U.S. Soccer Reset*, 2017, Dance to the Sun Publishers, LLC, p. 3.

57. http://www.uefa.com/

58. http://www.ussoccer.com/News/ Womens-National-Team/2011/06/ Reactions-after-the-US-WNT-Opens- 2011-World-Cup-with-2-0-Win.aspx

59. http://articles.nydailynews.com/2011– 07–16/ sports/29800900_1_abby- wambach-pia-sundhage-tibia-and-fibula

60. http://www.nytimes.com/2011/07/18/ sports/ soccer/japan-battles-back-to-win-women's-world-cup/ html?pagewanted=9112

61. http://www.fifa.com/tournaments/archive/ tournament=103/edition=4644/overview.html

62. *Soccer Tales III – Baba Yaga's Revenge*, Dance to the Sun Publishers, 2017, Epilogue – Sammie's Wrap-Up of 2015 Women's World Cup Final. pp. 55-58.

SOCCER TALES TRILOGY
ENDORSEMENTS

The book was given the endorsement of Mr. Fred Engh, CEO of the National Alliance of Youth Sports.

He called my story an "idyllic journey of joy and life's lessons through children's sports."

"I believe, as caring coaches, parents, and administrators of programs, it is our responsibility to ensure that every child enjoys a positive experience in whatever activity they choose. "Soccer Tales – Legend of the Shoelace Monster" is an idyllic journey of joy and teaches life's lessons through children's sports. It says a lot about sports and growing up."

Fred Eng
President and CEO
National Alliance of Youth Sport

The DiCicco Family of USWNT Coach Tony DiCicco give their Endorsement of the book:

Hi Lew,

I discussed the matter with my family and we decided that yes, you can dedicate the book to our father. Thank you for honoring him. It is a very fun book, nice job! Thank you for your kind words and thoughts.

Best of luck to you!

Alex DiCicco

BOOK REVIEW:

Soccer Tales – Legend of the Shoelace Monster
Posted by Rick Wolff on June 30, 2012

This is a delightful soccer fable that is written with great passion and joy from Lew Freimark. Although aimed for children, it's clearly written in a most unusual and fun manner – and along the way, it introduces the Shoelace Monster of the soccer pitch.

But this allegorical tale really is the story of Coach Stu and the wonderful time he has had coaching the Vipers through a number of seasons. Author Freimark is able to revisit the history of the game of soccer around the world, and in doing so, he provides a terrific history lesson for all soccer fans, young and old.

Best of all, the content is written in a light and clever approach – there's no sense of heavy-handedness that often accompanies kids' books. Bottom line – a fun and different kind of read.

by Taboola
Ask Coach Wolff · Copyright 2011 Pond Lane Productions, Inc. All Rights Reserved.

Follow "Ask Coach Wolff" WFAN RADIO

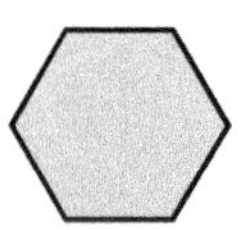

POSTSCRIPT

Nations come together every four years to play a World Cup of soccer. The United States is thought to be the next great cradle of soccer civilization. And who better to nurture the soccer babies, than the Shoelace Monster himself.

He comes from Brazil riding the musical notes and sounds of the rainforest, *DE JOAO, DE JOAO, EH, EH, EH.* Mellow sounds and a native song of rhythm beginning with a drumbeat and the echoing bang of a branch beating on a carved-out log

With shoelaces flying, ice cream soda armies doing battle and their own special brand of hilarity the Viper team of soccer players learn to love and play the world's game. Nothing can stop their energy and passion, not even an evil Referee and, her boss, the Big Commish. Watch out for the U.S. men's World Cup team in Qatar, 2022.

USSF SOCCER ELECTION

Datedline: February 10, 2018

US Soccer board member Carlos Cordeiro is elected new president of USSF soccer. Comments on Twitter were, with their Portuguese translation: *Booooooooooooooooooo!!!!! Booooo!!!!!!!! Booooo!!!!!! [Translated from Portuguese by Microsoft @MLS @ussoccer]*

A longtime executive at Goldman Sachs, Cordeiro has been the acting US Soccer vice president since 2016, and a member of the US Soccer Board since joining the federation in 2007 as an independent director.

LET'S GIVE HIM A CHANCE!!

Good Luck, Carlos.

* 9 7 8 0 9 9 9 3 1 1 0 5 9 *